P9-CQE-789

Here they come—puffing and grunting,

towels flapping, caps flying.

"Wait for me!" calls Little Bob.

His small green hands grip his

swimming tube tight.

The rains are over.

The waterhole is full. . . .

Tales from the
WATERHOLE

Bob Graham

CANDLEWICK PRESS
CAMBRIDGE, MASSACHUSETTS

Tales from the

Fruit Salad Swimsuit _____

Soccer Match _____

Daredevil Stunt _____

Vacation _____

Long Rains Party _____

WATERHOLE

For Oliver —
a smile that lights up the room

Copyright © 2004 by Bob Graham

First U.S. edition 2004

Library of Congress Cataloging-in-Publication Data is available.

Library of Congress Catalog Card Number 2003065224

ISBN 0-7636-2324-5

2 4 6 8 10 9 7 5 3 1

Printed in China

This book was typeset in Avenir Book.
The illustrations were done in watercolor, ink, pastel, and pencil.

Candlewick Press
2067 Massachusetts Avenue
Cambridge, Massachusetts 02140

visit us at www.candlewick.com

Fruit Salad Swimsuit

It was a warm, lazy evening.

Morris watched TV with his best friend, Billy.

Mom read her Dry Season mail-order catalog.

Dad snored.

"This is a lovely swimsuit. What do

you think, dear?" Mom asked Dad.

6

Dad raised an eyelid. "You look gorgeous in anything you wear," he said. Then he went back to sleep. He'd had a hard day lying in the sun. "Brrrrm," said Morris's little brother, Bob, under the table.

Two days later, Mom had her
new swimsuit.
"Well, what do you think, boys?
It's called Tropicana in the catalog,"
she said.
"You look beautiful, Mom,"
Morris said loudly.
Billy leaned toward Morris.
"Don't say it, Billy,"
said Morris out of the side
of his mouth.

But Billy whispered right into Morris's ear,

"Your mom looks like a fruit salad."

"You just wait, Billy," said Morris.

They went outside

and beat each

other up.

Well, they circled

and shuffled and grunted,

and they groaned and swished at the air.

Billy wound up on his shell,

and Morris had to help him up.

10

But, like all good friends,
they made up afterward.
"Have you two been fighting?"
asked Morris's mom.
"Not really," said Billy.
"It was nothing," said Morris.
Little Bob scribbled
with his finger in
the dust on
Billy's shell.

What color and style Morris's mom

brought to the waterhole!

Because they were friends, Billy said

nothing more about her looking

like a fruit salad.

And Morris said nothing about

Billy's mom looking a little like . . .

a rose garden.

SOCCER
MATCH

orris's sneakers squeaked

on the bathroom floor.

Morris sniffed.

The room smelled of powder, perfume,

and cod-flavored toothpaste.

14

"Mom, I'm going to mess around down
    at the waterhole," said Morris.
    Mom dabbed at her lipstick.
"Well, I'm going out for the afternoon,"
    she said, "so ask your father."
    She put a big wet kiss on his cheek.
"And take Little Bob with you," she added.

Morris went to find Dad.

Little Bob followed.

"Can I go to the waterhole?" Morris asked.

Dad stretched. Flies buzzed in the heat.

"You've got lipstick on your cheek, Morris."

"Oh," replied Morris. He smeared

at the spot. "Can I?"

"If you take Little Bob," Dad said.

"And be home by sundown."

17

On the way to the waterhole,

they met Billy.

"You brought a ball," said Billy.

"Yes," replied Morris.

He neatly swerved the ball

around Billy—who, being

a tortoise, was slow

on his feet.

"And you brought

Little Bob.

Hi, Bob,"

said Billy.

18

"Hello, Billy," said Little Bob shyly.

The remains of his lunch

were all down his front

(sardines and fries).

"Mucky, isn't he?" Billy said.

"Yeah, well . . . he's all right

sometimes," said Morris.

"Let's go."

19

Morris and Billy's friends were
kicking an old tin can around.
"Here's Morris!" yelled Leon Lion.
"He's got a ball," said Lucy Leopard.
"And a splotch on his cheek,"
grunted Harpo Hippo as
Morris arrived, puffing.

They picked teams.
(No one wanted Little Bob
or Slow Billy.)
But the two teams were soon
to become one, because . . .

21

22

over the hill came the moms!
They were returning very happily
from their afternoon together.
"SOCCER!" they yelled,
and tucked their skirts up high.

"Moms against the kids!"
said Morris's mom.
"Oh, no," groaned Morris.

23

Mrs. Elephant played goalie for the moms.

Billy, with Little Bob on his back for extra height,

played goalie for the kids.

Mrs. Elephant kicked off, then returned to the goal.

Mrs. Hippo took the ball upfield

in a spectacular run.

Morris's mom made a fine pass,

and Mrs. Giraffe headed it in for a—

"GOAL!" yelled the moms.

How they celebrated!

That goal was the first of many.

Slow Billy and Little Bob tried their best,

but the moms won 17–0.

It was no contest. Not really.

But while the moms were giving

the whole team a present

of big red splotchy kisses

(just like Morris's) . . .

Little Bob managed to roll the ball
into the moms' goal with his little feet.
"Goal!" he squeaked.
"17–1!" yelled Morris.
And the kids celebrated too.

DAREDEVIL
STUNT

It was a hot and busy afternoon.

Roars, grunts, squeaks, and squeals filled the air.

Morris was doing some tricky moves on his

skateboard, mainly to impress Wendy Warthog,

who was ignoring him completely.

"Look at me! I'm a jumbo jet!"
called Tessa Elephant
as she took off from
the diving board.

31

Tessa belly-flopped, and water
came down like a shower of rain.
"Tell you what I'll do," said Morris to Wendy.
"I'll do a STUNT."

Gerard Giraffe and Leon Lion

glanced at Morris.

Harpo Hippo turned his head.

Zoe Zebra moved for a better look.

And Wendy still ignored Morris.

As the pool settled, Morris went up on the bank.

"Here's my daredevil stunt!" he shouted.

"Harpo, Billy, and Little Bob, you get in the water.

Harpo, hold the diving board down.

When I come racing down, Harpo, you let go.
I will go up in the air and over the three of you . . .
and land on the other side."

A muffled snort came
from under Wendy's book.

Billy and Little Bob floated and waited.

Harpo held the diving board.

All was silent around the waterhole.

"Here he comes," squealed

Little Bob from his swimming tube.

From under her book,

Wendy took a tiny peek.

Morris hit the board at full speed—

just as a tickbird landed on Harpo's nose.

"AAAAACHOOOO!"

"Too early, too early!"
yelled Morris, who was
himself too late to stop.
Out of control,
he somersaulted high in the air,
once—

twice—

and landed in the soft mud.

SQUELCH!

But he got quickly to his feet

with a little skip and a jump.

Wendy put down her book.

"Not bad," she grunted.

"Needs a little more practice, though."

"It's the first time I have ever missed,"

said Morris.

"But it's the first time you've

ever tried," said Billy.

Morris gave him a stern look.

39

"My mom wants me home by sundown,"
said Wendy, gathering her things.
"We should all be getting home, then,"
said Morris, walking proudly.
Wendy had spoken to him—twice.

VACATION

Waldo Wildebeest was not happy.

"We're going on a walking vacation tomorrow."

He waved a hoof in the direction of the horizon.

"Oh, not good," replied Morris and Billy.

"We go every year," Waldo continued,

"with my zillions of relatives. We always

stop someplace boring to eat. I have to

watch all the little kids."

"Like I do with Little Bob?" Morris asked.

"Like about a hundred Little Bobs," said Waldo.

"The absolute worst thing,"

he went on, "is crossing the rivers.

All our stuff gets wet,

and my sneakers get muddy.

And I HATE IT!"

Morris had an idea.

43

He went home and asked his dad.

"What? The dinghy?" said Morris's dad.

"No, Waldo's family can't borrow it.

   I need it for my fishing."

"You never use it," said Mom.

   She slapped her tail once on the floor.

   So the dinghy went on Dad's back

   to the Wildebeests' house.

"It's for the river crossings," Morris said.

"Wicked!" said Waldo.

Morris's mom poked her husband in the back.

"Hmm . . . yes, well, just pull this cord and
she should start," said Dad.

"Let's have some tea," suggested Waldo's mom.

Morris's family sat down to tea and
ryegrass cakes with the Wildebeests.
There was a pause in the conversation.
"Any special plans for the vacation?"
Morris's dad asked.

Granddad Wildebeest replied,
"No, just eatin' . . . and walkin' . . .
and eatin' . . . and walkin'."
Waldo looked at Morris
and rolled his eyes.

The next morning, Morris, Billy, and Little Bob
watched Waldo's big family trudge past.
Waldo waved from inside a crowd of small
wildebeests. His old stroller carried the dinghy.
(It may carry him too, soon.)

48

"Would you feed our fish, Morris?"

 called Waldo's mom.

"Just a pinch a day."

"Sure," replied Morris.

"See you, Waldo."

49

The next day, at Waldo's house, Billy,
Morris, and Little Bob looked
at the tropical fish.
"Poor Waldo," said Billy.
"All those little kids to watch."
"Makes me feel almost—lucky!" said Morris.
He patted his brother's bumpy head
almost fondly.

LONG RAINS
PARTY

ld pants were quite OK

around the waterhole.

No pants, too.

Except for special occasions,

like the rains party.

"Look at you, Morris," said his mom.

"The long rains are coming, and you have

nothing for the party. These jeans

are so old, you can see through them.

We'll have to go shopping."

Morris slouched in despair.

He hated shopping.

At the store, Morris saw Gerard Giraffe.

"I have to get new jeans for the party," Gerard said miserably.

The assistant came over.

"These are our new Range Riders," she said. "They may be a bit short in the leg. . . ."

"He's long in the leg," said Gerard's mom.

"Takes after his father."

Morris's legs, on the other hand,

were so short, they could fit in

Gerard's pockets.

"Try these on, Morris,"
said his mom. "Never mind
the legs. It's the hole for the
tail that needs to be right."
Tall Gerard was well covered
by the changing-room doors.
But not Morris
(being so short in the leg).
"Do we have to do this?"
he asked.
"Of course," replied his mom.
"The Warthogs will have
Wendy dressed up pretty
as a picture."
"Oh . . ." said Morris.

56

"Hmm," said the moms.

They looked at each other.

"We can get the scissors out . . ."

said Morris's mom.

"And the sewing machine . . ."

said Gerard's mom

"Oh, no!" groaned Morris and Gerard.

"We'll take them," said the moms.

It was, of course, an obvious

solution to the problem.

A snip here.

A stitch there.

The pieces that came off the legs

of Morris's jeans . . .

went onto Gerard's.

And the whole thing was awful

for the two friends.

At the party, Wendy Warthog did indeed look as beautiful as an oil painting. Billy's shell sparkled, and Little Bob stayed clean for two whole minutes.

Billy's mom wanted to take a picture.

Gerard, Harpo, Tessa, Waldo, Zoe,

Lucy, Wendy, Leon, Morris, Billy

and Little Bob shuffled together.

"Where did you get those jeans, Morris?"

Wendy Warthog said out of the corner

of her mouth. "You look seriously cool!"

Morris blushed from his nose right

to the tip of his otherwise green tail.

"Er . . . thanks," he said.

"Smile, everyone!" Billy's mom called.

The camera clicked.

Some large black spots appeared in the dust.

The long rains had arrived.

A new season had begun.